KT-527-183

For my sister, Susan McIntosh.
An extraordinary kindergarten teacher,
who has been enchanting children for years.

First published 2005 by Walker Books Ltd
87 Vauxhall Walk, London SE11 5HJ

2 4 6 8 10 9 7 5 3 1

© 2005 Barney Saltzberg

The right of Barney Saltzberg to be identified as author/illustrator
of this work has been asserted by him in accordance
with the Copyright, Designs and Patents Act 1988

This book has been typeset in Blockhead Unplugged

Printed in China

All rights reserved. No part of this book may be reproduced, transmitted
or stored in an information retrieval system in any form or by any means,
graphic, electronic or mechanical, including photocopying, taping
and recording, without prior written permission from the publisher.

British Library Cataloguing in Publication Data:
a catalogue record for this book
is available from the British Library

ISBN 1-84428-230-9

www.walkerbooks.co.uk

THIS WALKER BOOK BELONGS TO:

____

____

____

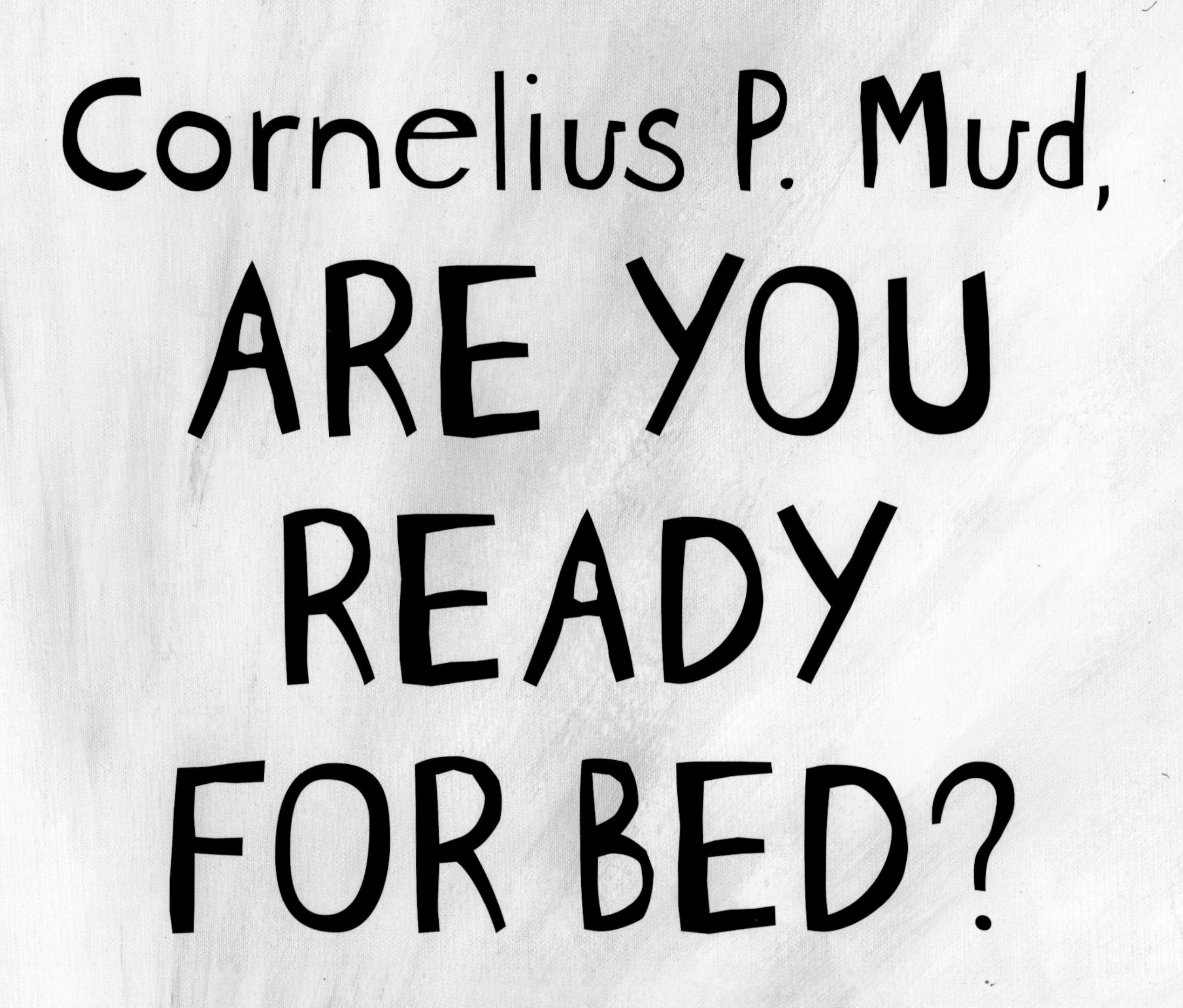

Cornelius P. Mud, ARE YOU READY FOR BED?

BARNEY SALTZBERG

WALKER BOOKS
AND SUBSIDIARIES
LONDON • BOSTON • SYDNEY • AUCKLAND

Cornelius P. Mud, do you know what time it is?

YES!

Have you put your toys away?

YES!

Have you fed your fish?

YES!

Have you used the toilet?

YES!

Have you brushed your teeth?

YES!

Have you put on your pyjamas?

YES!

Have you chosen a story?

YES!
GIVE A MOUSE A PIG
THE PIGGIES CRAWLED AWAY
MRS. MORGAN'S PIG
HAROLD AND THE PURPLE PIG
HEAVEN
ALL THE WAY HOME
Three not so little pigs
PIG BAD WOLF
CRAZY PIG DAY
WHERE THE WILD PIGS ARE

Are you ready
for bed?

NO!

Hmmm ... you've
put your toys away,
fed your fish,
used the toilet,
brushed your teeth,
put on your pyjamas
and chosen a story.

Have you forgotten
something?

YES!

A HUG!

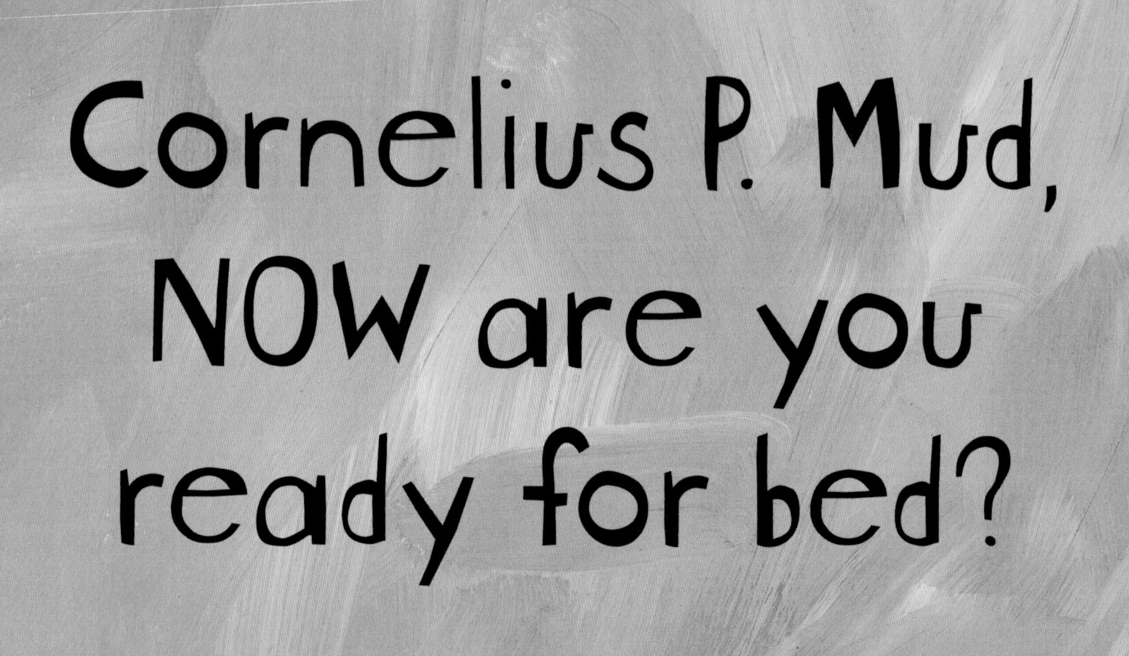

Cornelius P. Mud,
NOW are you
ready for bed?

HOGS & KISSES
HOGS & KISSES
MRS. MORGANS PIG
WHERE THE PIG ENDS
Charlottes Website
JAMES & THE GIANT PIG
YES!

Good night!

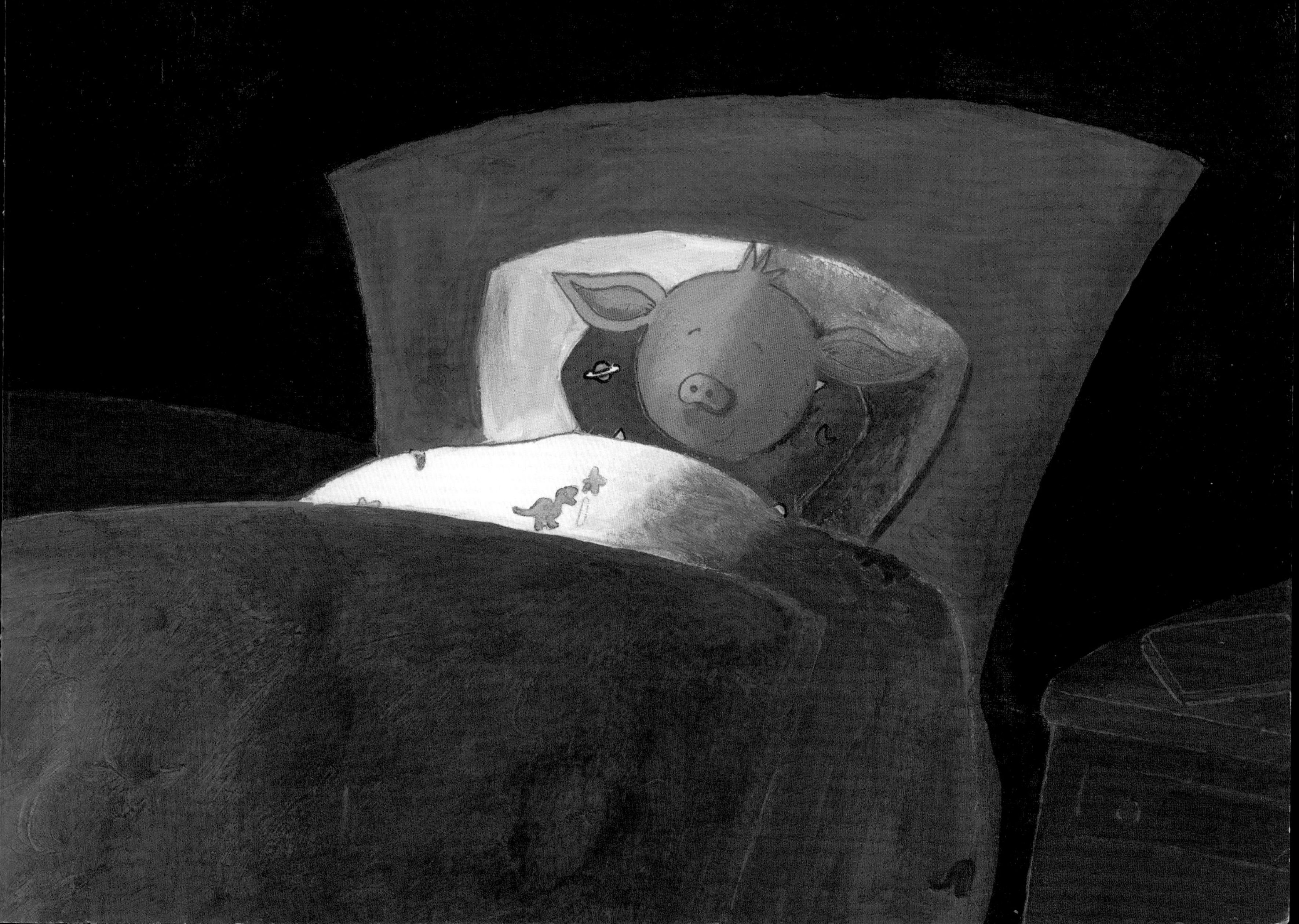

WALKER BOOKS is the world's leading
independent publisher of children's books.
Working with the best authors and illustrators
we create books for all ages, from babies
to teenagers – books your child will
grow up with and always remember. So...

FOR THE BEST CHILDREN'S BOOKS,
LOOK FOR THE BEAR